For Alexander
NW
To Moss with love
AA

VIKING
Published by the Penguin Group
Viking Penguin, a division of Penguin Books USA Inc.,
375 Hudson Street, New York, New York 10014, U.S.A.
Penguin Books Australia Ltd, Ringwood, Victoria, Australia
Penguin Books Canada Ltd, 2801 John Street, Markham, Ontario, Canada L3R 1B4
Penguin Books (N.Z.) Ltd, 182-190 Wairau Road, Auckland 10, New Zealand

First published in Great Britain by ABC, 1991
First American edition published in 1991

1 3 5 7 9 10 8 6 4 2

Text copyright © Nick Warburton, 1991
Illustrations copyright © Alex Ayliffe, 1991
The Author hereby asserts his moral right to be
identified as the Author of the work.

Library of Congress Catalog Card Number: 91-50393

ISBN 0-670-84155-2

Printed in Hong Kong

By **Nick Warburton**

Mr. Tite's Belongings

Illustrated by **Alex Ayliffe**

VIKING

Mr. Tite's belongings were everywhere: teetering on tables, balanced on chairs, bundled in cupboards, and littering the stairs.

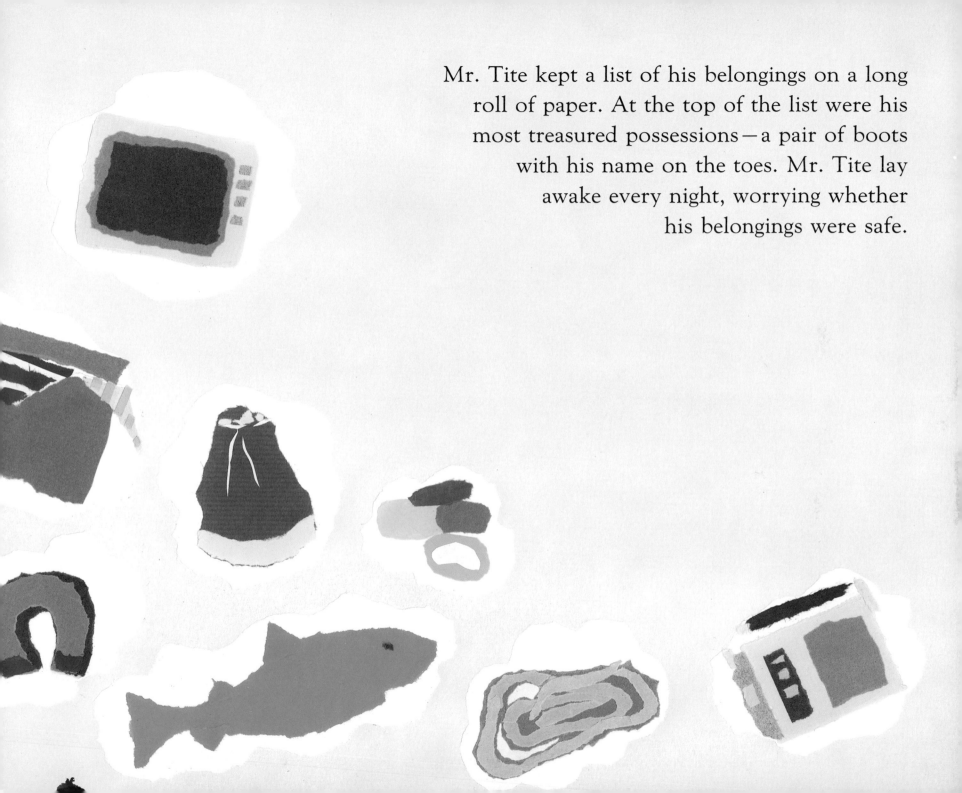

Mr. Tite kept a list of his belongings on a long roll of paper. At the top of the list were his most treasured possessions—a pair of boots with his name on the toes. Mr. Tite lay awake every night, worrying whether his belongings were safe.

Mr. Tite had a watchdog, Cheap, to guard his belongings. But he still couldn't sleep. "I need my belongings where I can see them," he thought.

So Mr. Tite and Cheap pushed and heaved everything into the bedroom.

But it was lumpy and uncomfortable on top of the pile, and Mr. Tite would be squashed underneath it. "This is no good," said Mr. Tite. "My belongings are safe—but where can I sleep?"

In the morning, Mr. Tite bought a spade. He added
it to his list, then started to dig a hole in his garden.

Cheap helped. He was a very good digger.
It took them all day to dig the pit.
"Soon my belongings will be safe
underground," thought Mr. Tite.

That night, Mr. Tite perched his bed on top of the pile,
so he could keep watch until everything was safely buried.
But the bed wobbled, and Mr. Tite couldn't get to sleep.

It took a long time to bury the pile. Mr. Tite replanted his flowers then stood back to have a look.

"This won't do," groaned Mr. Tite. "They're my flowers and they should be safely underground, not sticking out so everyone can see. And there's nowhere to hide my spade, either."

Mr. Tite dug his things up again.
When they were all out, he sat on top of them and thought.
"I know the very place!" he cried at last. "A nice dark cave,
far from other people. My things *must* be safe there!"

Mr. Tite and Cheap loaded the belongings onto the
bed and secured them with rope.
   Then Mr. Tite put on his favorite boots. Finally
he tied his gate onto the bed. "It's mine, so I
must be sure it's safe."

All night, they pushed the bed — through the dark streets,
out of town, into the country, until they came to a tunnel.
Mr. Tite tried to squash his belongings as flat as he could.
But the bed wouldn't fit through the tunnel.

He took off the gate.

"Maybe I won't need a gate in a cave," he said.

But the bed wouldn't go through the tunnel until they had removed the gate, a soap dish, four buckets, a tennis racket, a box of purple socks and an armchair.

Mr. Tite wasn't happy.

A mile up the road they saw a cave in a mountain.
But to get to the cave, they had to cross a rickety
wooden bridge over a foaming river.
Mr. Tite pushed the bed a little way onto
the bridge. The bridge began to creak.
Mr. Tite took off a pencil and
pushed the bed again.
The bridge creaked loudly.
He removed a bright blue
plastic shark and pushed
the bed — but the
bridge still creaked.

Bit by bit, they took everything off.
Mr. Tite pushed the empty bed onto the bridge.
The bridge still gave a little creak.
"Now what?" sobbed Mr. Tite. "I've taken
everything off and the bridge still creaks."
But he knew what he had to do.

He stepped onto the bridge without the bed.
There was a tiny creak.
Mr. Tite sighed.
Only his two most treasured possessions were left.

He unlaced his precious boots and tossed them away.
He stepped onto the bridge.

There was not even the tiniest creak.

Mr., Tite walked barefoot across the bridge
to the other side.

"Hurray, hurray!" he shouted.

He was so happy that he scruffed up the hair
under Cheap's chin.
Mr. Tite had never done anything like that before.
They danced until they were out of breath.
Then they sat down on the grass and looked around.

"It's beautiful here," said Mr. Tite.
He lay back yawning.
"The grass is softer than my bed and feels cool between my toes."
Mr. Tite smiled and fell fast asleep.